The BEAR Who Slept Through CHRISTMAS

Story by
John Barrett
Illustrations by
Rick Reinert Productions
Developed by
The LeFave Company

℗ CHILDRENS PRESS, CHICAGO

ISBN 0-89542-942-X 295

While the rest of the world is getting ready for Christmas, bears are getting ready for bed.

In fact, from a quarter till Winter until about half-past Spring, bears do nothing but sleep . . . hibernate, we call it.

Most bears have never heard of Christmas.

WELCOME TO BEARBANK

Henry Bear was sleepy even on a wide-awake day. But now that Fall was here, Henry was **very** tired. If it hadn't been for his roommate, Henry probably wouldn't have been able to wake up for work.

Ted Edward Bear was Henry's roommate. Ted was a different sort of bear. He had an inquiring mind. In other words, he was curious. The thing that made Ted curious was Christmas.

"Henry, have you ever heard of something called 'Christmas'?" Ted asked.

Ted E. Bear first read about Christmas in a book at Grizzly University. He tried to explain it to his friend Henry:

"There is this place called 'Christmas' where you hear beautiful music and you find wonderful gifts.

"There's a big human with a white beard and a red suit. He's in charge of Christmas. Isn't that amazing, Henry?"

"ZZZZZZZZ."

Henry did not have an inquiring mind.

The other bears laughed!

"Are you kidding?" giggled Foster Bear, "A big red human?"

"You're a silly dreamer," sighed Patti Bear.

But Ted went right on dreaming. He dreamed of being the first bear to find Christmas. "This could be as important as Admiral Bear's discovery of the East Pole," Ted declared.

Unfortunately, Ted was dreaming when he should have been working.

Ted's boss was furious. "Explain this mess!" he yelled.

"Well, sir," Ted began, "I was thinking about Christmas and the honey sort of got away from me."

The owner of the Organic Honeyworks fumed, "A bear should not think about two things at once! I didn't get where I am by thinking!"

"I know," agreed Ted. "But Christmas is supposed to be a wonderful place. There are lights and music and a big human in a red suit . . ."

"Then go find it," Ted's boss interrupted, "and wherever it is, stay there!"

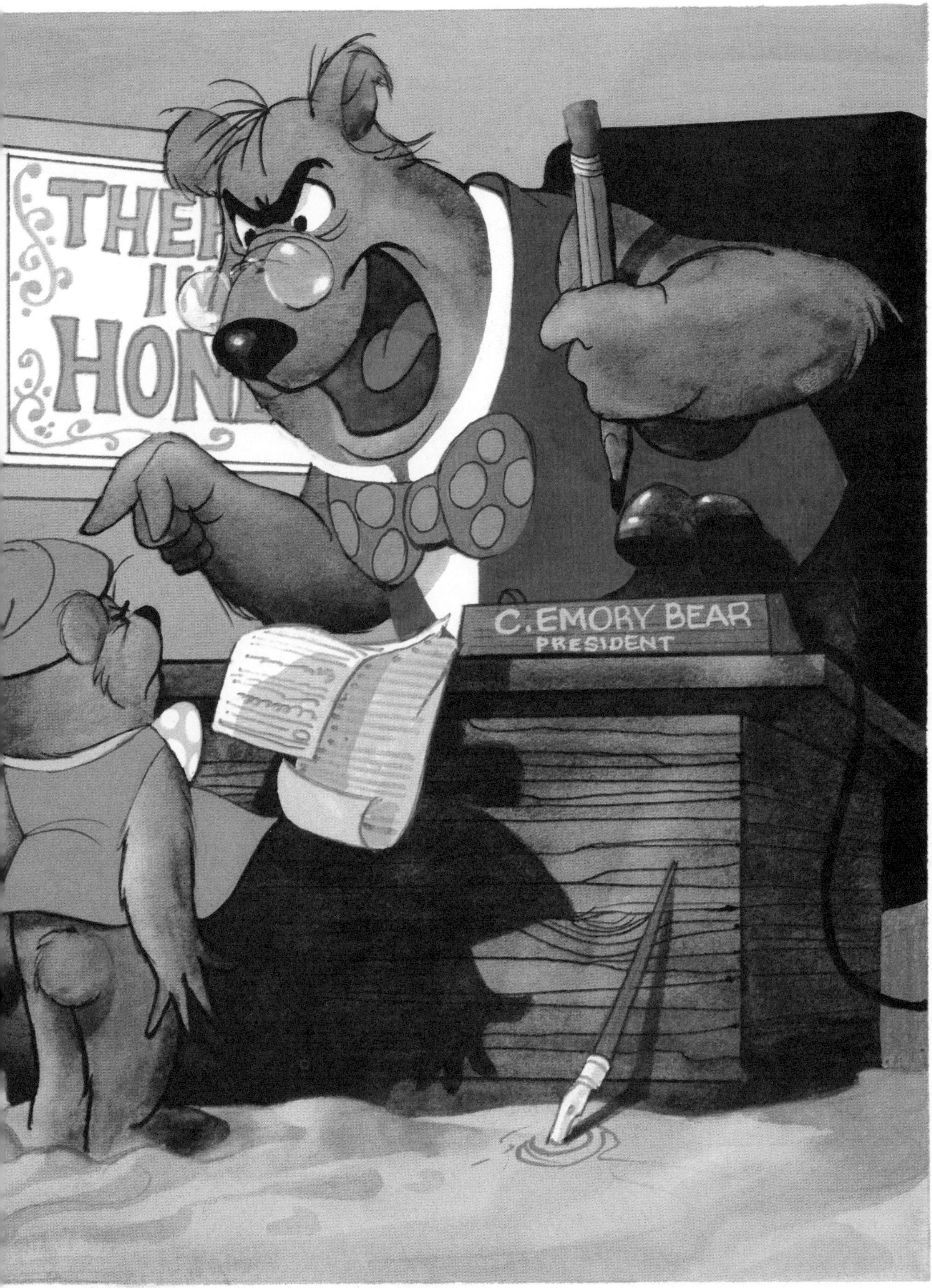
C. EMORY BEAR
PRESIDENT

Ted E. Bear studied the airline schedules. He hoped a flight might take him to Christmas.

"Where would you like to go?" asked the Bear Air ticket clerk.

"I'd like to fly to Christmas," Ted answered, ". . . or at least a nearby airport."

The ticket bear stared at Ted. He began to laugh. The laughter grew to a roar.

He shouted to the line of waiting bears, "We've got a bear who wants to go to Christmas!"

More bears laughed.

While the rest of the bears flew off on Winter hibernation vacations, Ted E. Bear set out on foot to find Christmas.

One sleepy evening, Ted climbed over a hill and saw a brightly lit city. His heart jumped. "I must be getting close to Christmas," he said.

When he reached the city, Ted tried to talk to several passersby. He shouted, but the cars and people made so much noise, nobody heard the little bear.

"Wait! What's that?"

Ted cocked his little bear head. Over the noise of the traffic, he heard beautiful music. The sound came from a magnificent building. Ted scrambled up the steps and looked inside. A choir sang. The young bear decided it must be the music of Christmas.

"If I can hear the music," Ted thought, "Christmas must be very close by."

His heart beat faster.

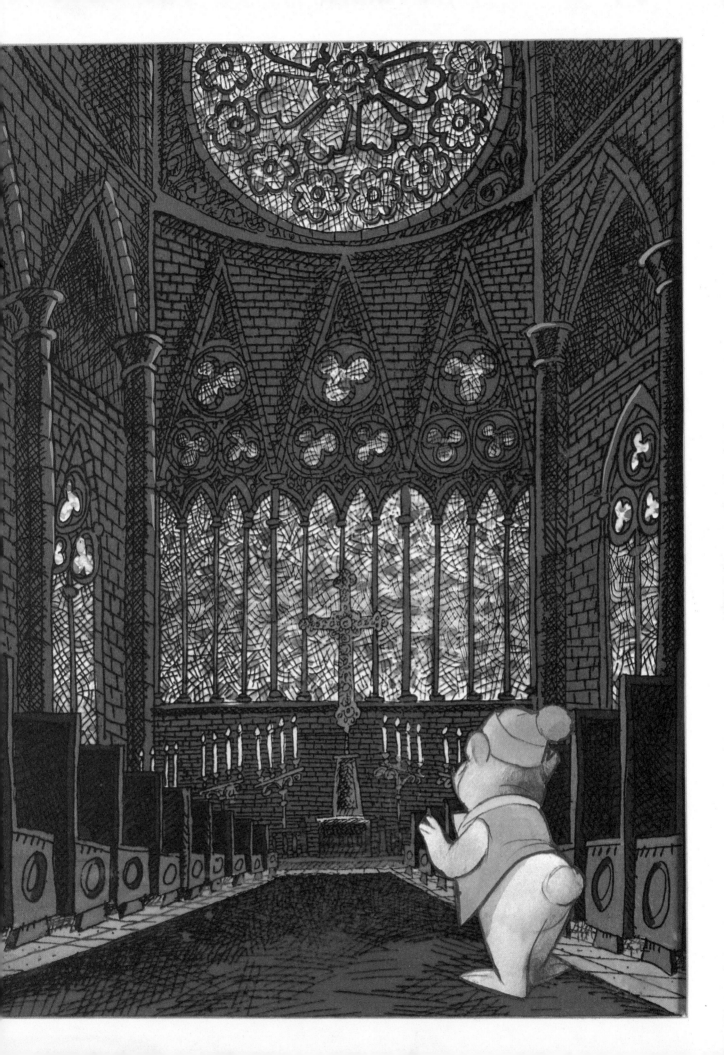

He rubbed his sleepy eyes and walked down a busy street. He glanced in a store window and stopped in amazement. The store was full of the most wonderful gifts the young bear had ever seen. "There are the gifts!" Ted said aloud.

He pushed open the door and climbed into the store window to talk with the toys. "Is this the place where Christmas is?" Ted asked eagerly.

"Not here," a toy soldier said and saluted smartly.

Ted was confused.

Ted turned to a pretty dancing doll and said, "I heard the music, and you are the most beautiful gifts I have ever seen. How far away can Christmas be?"

"It's very close," the doll replied, "but somebody must buy us before the store closes or we'll have to go back to the stockroom for a whole year."

Ted noticed a little girl looking in the store window at him. "What about her?" he asked.

"I don't think she can afford us," said the soldier.

Ted heard the click of a lock and the lights in the store began to go off.

"Oh no!" cried the doll.

Ted was trapped in a store where Christmas wasn't. He tried every door and window. Then, back in the stockroom where the toys would have to go until next Christmas, Ted spied a window.

He reached . . .

   and stretched . . .

      and climbed . . .

and he tumbled out into an alley.

Ted picked himself up, dashed to the street and ka-bump! He ran smack into a big human wearing a red suit. Ted E. Bear was wide-eyed with wonder. He held his hat politely and said, "I am looking for a place called 'Christmas.' Can you help me?'

The man in the red suit held Ted in his arms. "My goodness," he chuckled, "do you realize you'd be the very first bear to ever find Christmas?"

"Yes, sir," Ted nodded.

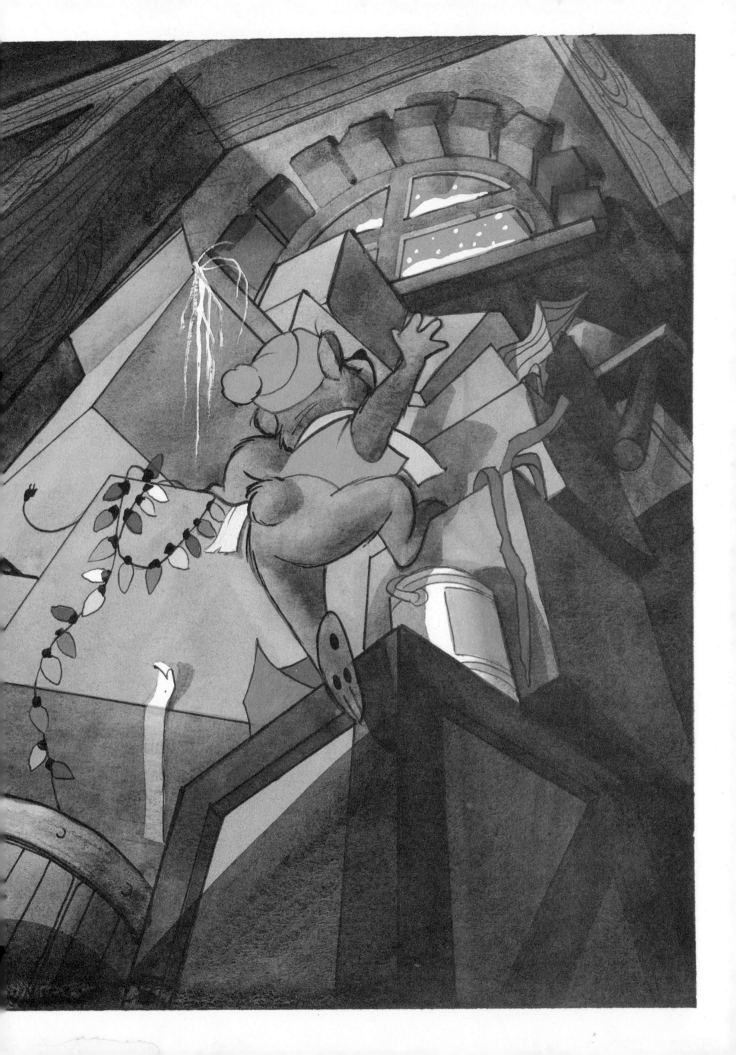

"Well then," said the kind gentleman, "let me explain: Christmas is a way of giving, it is a way of sharing . . . a way of loving."

Ted appeared puzzled. "You mean it isn't in a place?"

The man smiled. "It is, little bear," he said warmly, "but the place is in your heart."

Ted frowned a tired frown. "That's very hard for a bear to understand," he said.

"It is hard for people to understand," said the gentleman. He handed Ted a note. "Here," he said. "this is an address where you'll find Christmas."

Tired Ted E. Bear thanked the man and walked down the street. The building at the address didn't seem to be anything special. "Can this be the right address?" Ted wondered. He looked up. A few lights flickered in the window above. He climbed the stairs to the house.

Ted E. Bear stood in the room with the lighted tree. He yawned and looked about. The gifts weren't nearly as wonderful as those in the store. And there was no music. "There must be a mistake," Ted said aloud. The little bear was very tired. All the rest of the bears had been asleep for weeks. Ted crawled under the tree to rest, just for a minute.

As he rested, a door opened. A little girl tiptoed into the room. It was the same little girl who had looked at Ted through the store window. Her eyes opened wide and sparkled with a happy tear. "A little bear," she whispered. She reached down and lifted Ted in her arms.

And suddenly . . .

The air was filled with beautiful music!
The lights on the tree shimmered!
Ted Edward Bear found Christmas!